Where Is Bear?

An Animal Friends Reader

by **Liza Charlesworth**
illustrated by **Ian Smith**

Text copyright © 2015 by Liza Charlesworth
Illustrations copyright © 2015 Scholastic Inc.

All rights reserved. Published by Scholastic Inc., *Publishers since 1920*. SCHOLASTIC and associated logos are trademarks and/or registered trademarks of Scholastic Inc.

The publisher does not have any control over and does not assume any responsibility for author or third-party websites or their content.

No part of this publication may be reproduced, stored in a retrieval system, or transmitted in any form or by any means, electronic, mechanical, photocopying, recording, or otherwise, without written permission of the publisher. For information regarding permission, write to Scholastic Inc., Attention: Permissions Department, 557 Broadway, New York, NY 10012.

This book is a work of fiction. Names, characters, places, and incidents are either the product of the author's imagination or are used fictitiously, and any resemblance to actual persons, living or dead, business establishments, events, or locales is entirely coincidental.

ISBN: 978-0-545-85969-1

10 9 8 7 6 5 4 3 2 1   18 19 20 21 22/0

Printed in Malaysia   106
First printing 2015

Book design by Maria Mercado

W9-AZH-158

SCHOLASTIC INC.

Where is Bear?
It is her birthday!

Is Bear at the pond?
No.

But flowers are there!
The friends get some
flowers for Bear.

Is Bear at the bush?
No.

But berries are there!
The friends get some
berries for Bear.

Is Bear at the hive?
No.

But honey is there!
The friends get some
honey for Bear.

The friends have flowers
and berries and honey.
But where is Bear?

It starts to rain.
Plop, plop, plop.

So the friends run into a cave.

Surprise!
Bear is there.

"Happy birthday!" they say. Bear gets flowers and berries and honey.

"Thank you," said Bear.
"I will share."